UNDERWORLD

SIMON CHESHIRE

Underworld ISBN 978-1-78147-805-9

Text © Simon Cheshire 2014
Complete work © Badger Publishing Limited 2014

Publisher: Susan Ross
Senior Editor: Danny Pearson
Publishing Assistant: Claire Morgan
Copyeditor: Cheryl Lanyon
Designer: Bigtop Design Ltd

2 4 6 8 10 9 7 5 3 1

CHAPTER 1

"I saw it!" she said. "I tell you, I saw it."

"Saw what?" asked Joe's mum.

"Some sort of animal," said Mrs Burke.

It was Monday morning, just after eight o'clock. Joe and his mum were leaving home. Joe was on his way to school. His mum was on her way to work at the local supermarket.

Mrs Burke lived next door to them, at number 77. She knew their normal routine, so she was waiting on her doorstep to stop them as they left the house.

"I just wondered if you'd seen it?" she said to Joe and his mum. "This animal?"

"When was this?" asked Joe.

"Last night," said Mrs Burke. "About half past eleven. I was just going to bed. I looked out the front here. I always take a look out the front last thing at night. And I saw it. Over there."

She pointed across the road. Opposite the houses was a large stretch of grass. Beyond that were trees. This was Oakshot Wood. Oakshot Road, where Joe lived, snaked around the wood and led down to the centre of town.

"By the trees?" asked Joe.

"Yes," said Mrs Burke. "It ran along the edge of the wood. Well, no, not ran. Not ran, exactly. It more sort of hopped."

"What was it, a kangaroo?" laughed Joe.

"It's no laughing matter," said Mrs Burke. "It scared the life out of me. It was about a metre high. Not very tall. It was kind of stooped over. I was so scared because I've never seen anything like that before. That's why I thought I'd ask you if you'd seen it too."

"It must have been a dog," said Joe's mum. "Something like that."

"No, no," said Mrs Burke. "It was on its hind legs. It was sort of walking, sort of hopping. What's the word I want? Lolloping, that's it. Swaying a bit. Rather like you see monkeys walk."

"Well it can't have been an ape," said Joe's mum. "We'd have heard if something had escaped from somewhere."

"And there are no zoos or wildlife parks for miles," said Joe.

Mrs Burke shook her head. "I don't know. I really don't know. It scared me half to death. It definitely wasn't a monkey or a dog. I only saw its shape. It had funny-shaped ears. And its arms were kind of bent up."

"Sorry, we've got to go," said Joe's mum. "We'll be late."

"Oh, yes, sorry Mrs Harris, I don't want to keep you," smiled Mrs Burke. "I just thought I'd ask."

Joe and his mum hurried away.

"She must be going a bit batty," whispered Joe's mum.

Joe shrugged. "Just a dog or something. After all, it was night. The street lamps aren't exactly bright!"

"Her eyesight must be going," added his mum.

They parted at the corner of Walker Street. Joe's mum went left towards the supermarket. Joe carried on along Oakshot Road.

A hundred metres on he came to a roadblock. Police were diverting cars. People on foot were being led around the block in small groups by police officers.

The reason for the roadblock was a noisy demo. A large group of locals, holding placards and chanting slogans, was marching across Oakshot Road. They were heading towards the wood.

Joe saw some pupils from his school. They were watching the protesters march while they waited for the police to escort them past the demo. Joe walked over to them.

"Hi," he said. "Is this about the fracking?"

"Yes," nodded a boy from his year group. "They're drilling again today."

Joe could hear the steady whine of the drills. It was coming from inside Oakshot Wood. A mining company had been drilling into the ground there for more than a month. They were mining for shale gas by pumping water into rocks deep underground.

Joe checked his watch. "I hope this isn't going to take long."

"They're right to protest!" said a voice behind him.

He turned to find Sarah Jones. She also lived in Oakshot Road, a few doors along from Joe. She was in his tutor group at school, but the two of them had never got on well. Joe was a quiet, laid-back guy, with a small circle of friends. Sarah was sporty and opinionated, always first with her hand up in class.

"OK," shrugged Joe.

"No, it's not OK," said Sarah. "Fracking is dangerous. It pollutes water supplies, for one thing."

"And," said Joe, "if these test holes they're drilling work out, it will also bring hundreds of jobs to the town."

"At the expense of the environment," said Sarah. "Oakshot Wood is historic woodland."

Joe was getting cross now. He felt like arguing, just for the sake of it. "Fracking takes place all over the world. It's no worse than coal mining or drilling for oil. You'd be the first to complain if the gas ran out and your central heating got turned off."

Sarah was about to reply, but didn't. Instead she shook her head angrily and stormed off.

"I think it's going to be one of those days," muttered Joe to himself.

The police led Joe and the others around the protest. They continued on their way to school. Joe thought no more about the fracking, or about what Mrs Burke had seen.

However, on his way home that day, he passed a horrible sight.

CHAPTER 2

On the edge of Oakshot Wood, opposite Joe's house, a group of kids from the nearby primary school was gathered. Joe paid them no attention at first. Then he overheard what they were saying.

"Eugh, that's gross!"

"It must have been dead for days!"

Puzzled, he crossed the grass and approached them. "What's up?" he asked.

The kids parted to reveal a stinking carcass.

It was a large, ginger cat. It had been ripped open from neck to tail. Most of its innards had gone. Its eyes stared glassily and its mouth hung open.

"Oh yuk!" cried Joe. "Where did that come from?"

"Samson dragged it out of the wood!" said one of the kids. A border collie sat panting at the boy's feet. "He didn't kill it, he just found it. Where do you think its guts have gone?"

"Maybe a badger ate them," said Joe, wrinkling his nose. He turned away from the blood and the smell and went home.

The dead cat stayed on his mind all evening. What would have slashed the poor creature like that? It looked as if it had been opened up like a school lunchbox!

*

Two things happened in the next few days. Both of them made Joe think about the cat, and also about the strange 'animal' that Mrs Burke had said she'd spotted. The first was a report in the local paper. Joe's mum pointed it out to him. It said:

Oakshot Woods resident claims 'goblin' sighting

Locals living in the Oakshot Woods area have already complained of noise and disruption caused by the current controversial fracking operation. Now they have a new nuisance to contend with: a mysterious 'goblin' sighted by Hillside Grove resident Mr John Spears.

Mr Spears, 45, claims he saw a strange creature going through his bin on Tuesday night.

"I heard a noise in the alley behind the house shortly before midnight," he states. "I went out there, thinking I'd have to scare a fox away. But I found a hideous, dwarfish creature rooting through the waste food wheelie bin."

He continues: "When I disturbed it, it looked straight at me. It had an evil-looking face, with big, pointed ears and large, white eyes. It was horrible. Then it ran off into the dark."

Mr Spears, an employee at SuperSave, claims he'd had nothing to drink. He also claims he is not prone to imagination or to seeing things. "I know what I saw," he asserts. "It looked just like some kind of storybook goblin."

"That guy's in charge of the cooked meat counter at work," said his mum. "He's been talking about this thing for days."

"It must be the same animal Mrs Burke saw," said Joe. "Weird."

"It seems she was right after all. I wonder what it was?" said his mum.

"I bet someone around here has got some sort of exotic pet," said Joe. "A sloth or some sort of small primate that has got out of its cage. Probably illegal, which is why it hasn't been reported missing."

The second thing that happened was that Sarah Jones called at Joe's house the following evening. She'd hardly spoken to him since Monday morning so he was amazed to see her on his doorstep. She was handing out A4 photocopies.

"Our dog's gone missing," she said. She handed Joe one of the photocopies. It showed a photo of a black Labrador and details of a reward. "Have you seen her wandering around?"

"No, sorry," said Joe.

Sarah seemed very upset. Joe felt sorry for her.

"Has she gone missing before?" he asked.

"No, never," said Sarah. "That's what's so strange. She's a very calm, loyal dog. She never wanders off. She was in her kennel in the garden overnight on Tuesday. Next morning she was gone. My parents say they heard a noise in the night, like scuffling, but didn't think anything of it."

"Was the garden secure?"

"There's a locked gate and a high fence," said Sarah. "Neither was damaged. She couldn't have jumped over them, it's impossible, they're far too high. She'd have to be carried over."

"Weird," said Joe.

"Our neighbour's cat has vanished too," said Sarah. "A big, old ginger thing. That disappeared last week."

Joe frowned. He didn't tell Sarah about what those kids had found. "Would you like me to help look for your dog?"

Now it was Sarah's turn to frown. "You? Why?"

Joe felt embarrassed. "There are some odd things happening around here. I just want to help."

At first, Sarah was wary of his offer. She wasn't sure if he was being straight with her or not.

In the end her concern for her missing dog overcame her doubts.

"OK, you can help me put these photocopies through a few doors," she said. "And I was going to take a look in Oakshot Woods. We often took her for a walk in there."

It was getting dark. The dull streetlights blinked on.

Joe and Sarah gave out the rest of the photocopies. Some of them they stuck to lampposts with sticky tape. They called at the corner shop and had one put in the window.

By the time they got around to visiting Oakshot Woods, the sun had been set for over an hour. It was gloomy on the grass beside Oakshot Road, but inside the wood itself was almost pitch black. Joe and Sarah could barely see more than a few metres ahead.

"Let's go back," said Joe.

"No," said Sarah. "We're here now, scaredy cat."

"Why don't we come back with flashlights?" suggested Joe.

"We'll just go a little bit further."

Twigs cracked under their shoes. Joe could smell rotting leaves and decayed bark. Soon they came to a long, wire fence. Behind it, a large area had been cleared of trees.

"That's where the fracking's happening," said Joe. "Well, we can't go any further."

They peered through the fence. Drilling had ended for the day. The mining company had locked up the entire site until the morning. The only lights were security lamps, rigged up outside temporary cabins, and stacks of mining equipment. A couple of small lorries stood tall and silent in the darkness.

Sarah sighed. "Come on then, we'll head home."

They turned and walked back the way they had come.

Suddenly, Joe stopped in mid-step. "Shh! What was that?"

They listened. The wood was dark and motionless.

"What was what?" asked Sarah.

"Sorry, I thought I heard a sort of scratching sound," said Joe.

They continued walking. A few metres further on the sound came again. They both heard it this time. A soft scuffling sound. It was like an animal rooting through the undergrowth, or something dragging across the carpet of fallen leaves.

They turned slowly. They looked all around, peering into the night. Their eyes were used to the dark now, but they couldn't see anything moving.

There it was again! The same sound. Closer now.

Sarah whispered, "Someone's behind us."

Without moving their feet so that they wouldn't make any noise at all, they twisted to look behind them. A few metres away, the scuffling sent a flurry of leaves scattering across the ground.

They almost jumped out of their skins.

Slowly, very slowly, something began to come out from behind a tree. All they could see was a shape. It was short, almost squat. It walked on spindly legs. Its arms were short, twisted, and ended in long, sharp claws. Its head was gnarled and hairless with triangular, pointed ears. Its mouth was a lipless, shuddering split. Its eyes were wide, round and completely white except for tiny black pupils at the centre.

Joe's head was filled with only one word: goblin!

CHAPTER 3

Joe and Sarah hardly dared to breathe. The creature, the goblin, was only a few metres away from them. Its head swayed slightly from side to side. Its upturned nose twitched.

"I think it's sniffing us out," whispered Sarah.

The creature suddenly turned to face in their direction.

"It heard you whisper," breathed Joe, as quietly as he could.

"Let's… go…" breathed Sarah.

The creature took a step towards them. Instantly, Joe and Sarah both let out a yell of fright. They spun on their heels and ran. Their footsteps crunched against the leafy ground. Behind them, they could hear the goblin running after them.

"It's chasing us!" cried Sarah.

"Maybe it wasn't a good idea to run," gasped Joe. "Maybe you're supposed to face goblins down. You know, like tigers. Or is it bears?"

"Who cares! Just run!"

The edge of the wood was in sight. The goblin suddenly gave an eerie, high-pitched screech. The sound of it right behind them almost sent Joe and Sarah tumbling over in shock.

They reached the last line of trees. Ahead of them was the wide, grassy area. Beyond that were the houses of Oakshot Road.

Sarah flashed a glance over her shoulder. "It's getting closer!"

More sounds were coming from the wood. Rustling and cracking, like an army on the march. The goblin's wailing cry was answered by another, from deep inside the wood.

"There's more of them!" yelled Joe.

By now, Joe and Sarah were racing across Oakshot Road. They dared not look back. They dashed into Joe's house.

"What on earth is going on?" asked Joe's mum. "Joe? Hello, er, Sarah isn't it? From down the road? You both look as if you've seen a ghost!"

Neither of them answered her. Joe hurried to the big window in the living room which overlooked the wood.

"Look!" he cried. "They're just waiting."

Sarah and Joe's mum stood close to the window. Their breath fogged the glass.

"How many of them are there?" asked Sarah.

Joe's mum simply stared, open-mouthed.

"Must be at least twenty," said Joe. "Look, there are more crawling out past the trees."

A large group of the creatures was gathered on the grass. They had stopped chasing after their new, human prey. Instead, they were looking around warily and sniffing the air.

"They're not used to being out in the open," said Joe.

"It won't hold them back for long, though," said Sarah. "Remember, one of them went through that man's bin. He's in Hillside Grove, and that's one street further along than we are."

All along the row of houses, curtains and blinds were being pulled aside. People had heard the strange cries of the goblins. Joe and Sarah's neighbours were looking out at the creatures, hardly believing their eyes. Most of them had the same expression on their faces as Joe's mum.

"W-w-we'd better call the police," she said.

"And say what?" muttered Joe.

At that moment, Mrs Burke appeared on the other side of the road. She was walking home up Oakshot Road. She'd been to a public meeting about the fracking at the nearby Community Centre. She kept her eyes on the pavement ahead of her. She didn't notice the group of goblins about thirty metres away on the grass.

As soon as he saw her, Joe ran out of the house. Sarah followed him.

"Mrs Burke!" he called, at the top of his voice. "Come this way! Quickly! Over here!"

She hadn't heard him.

"Mrs Burke!" yelled Joe and Sarah together. "Turn this way! You're going towards – "

It was too late. The creatures were suddenly alert, sniffing. Crawling and scuttling across the grass, they closed in on Mrs Burke.

She screamed as the first one pounced. It knocked her to the ground. Others leaped forwards.

"We've got to scare them off!" said Joe.
"But how?"

"What about light?" said Sarah. "These things haven't been seen during the day, and that one in the woods didn't appear to see us. Maybe that's why they stayed on the grass, they didn't like the street lamps?"

Joe fetched a couple of flashlights, kept in the cupboard under the stairs in case of power cuts. He gave one to Sarah and the two of them hurried out into the street.

"Joe! Don't go out there!" yelled his mum.

Joe and Sarah aimed at the creatures. The flashlights were powerful enough to send beams right across the road. At once, the goblins flinched and turned away.

"You were right!" said Joe. "Keep sweeping the beams across them."

It took only a few minutes to send the creatures scurrying back to the woods. They dragged Mrs Burke along with them.

CHAPTER 4

By the next morning, the police had roped off most of Oakshot Wood. The mining company was allowed to carry on drilling. The official story given to the media by the police was that the creatures were a hoax. A film company was staging a viral marketing campaign to promote a new movie. The police would find those responsible and prosecute them for causing a nuisance.

"Idiots!" said Sarah. "Everyone on our section of Oakshot Road saw those things! What about poor Mrs Burke?"

Joe and Sarah met in the school canteen at lunchtime. "They're saying she was paid to play along with their hoax," said Joe. "Yes, it's a stupid explanation. However, to be fair, which explanation sounds more likely: that it was a stunt, or that it really was weird creatures from the woods? The police must be taking it seriously, on the quiet, or they wouldn't have roped off the woods. On the way to school, I saw more police being posted outside the drilling site."

Sarah sighed. "I'm going to the public library after school. I'm going to do some research. We have to find out what those creatures are and where they came from. Why have they suddenly appeared like this?"

As the sun set that day, Sarah called at Joe's house. When Joe opened the front door, he heard the distant sound of the mining company's drills.

"They're working late," he said.

"They're due to get the first supplies of gas out of the site tonight," said Sarah. "The media and the local MP are there to see it. The mining company wants lots of publicity."

Sarah was carrying a bundle of files and papers. They spread them out on the dining room table.

"What did you find?" asked Joe.

"The truth, I think," said Sarah. She slid papers and photocopies across to Joe as she spoke. "I've spent hours looking back through local archives. The library has newspapers going back to 1789. They also have other records made by people living in this area, going back to the Middle Ages. This is a newspaper cutting from 1955. Notice anything familiar about it?"

The cutting began:

Farmer disturbed by unusual sights and sounds

The tenants at Oakshot Farm have been alarmed on a number of recent nights by strange events in and around the farm's buildings. Mr Biggs, the farmer, is said to have encountered intruders in his barn on no less than three occasions. These intruders were, says Mr Biggs, of the animal variety.

"They weren't like any animal I've ever seen before," he told our reporter yesterday. "They walked on two thin legs and they made a horrible, wailing cry. They looked like something from a horror story. One of them went after a couple of my chickens."

"This is just like the newspaper article from last week," said Joe. "But where's Oakshot Farm? I've never heard of it."

"It doesn't exist any more. These houses we live in were built on the land in the 1960s. Now look at this. It's another press report, this time from 1820."

The headline read:

Workmen digging cellars flee in terror: they report pursuit by hideous goblins

"They were building the original farmhouse that stood where Oakshot Road is today," said Sarah.

"They said they were chased away by monsters. One of them became a nervous wreck and went to live abroad. Another was caught by the creatures and was never seen again."

Joe looked at the cutting. It included a drawing made by one of the workmen. It showed a creature very like the ones from the wood.

"And here," said Sarah, giving him another sheet of paper. "This is dated 1690. They were clearing part of the wood to make room for cattle pasture. People refused to come near this place after several locals vanished. They said it was haunted by evil spirits."

"So these creatures have been seen, on and off, for centuries," said Joe. "But why now? And why then? Why did they appear at those particular times?"

"I think I know that, too," said Sarah. "In 1955, the main road past town was being built. There was a report about it in the same newspaper. A huge section was cut out of the hill beside the wood so the road could run straight and level. In 1820, big holes would have been dug right where we are now to create cellars for a large farmhouse. In 1690, they'd have been chopping down huge, heavy trees. Do you see the connection?"

"Each time, they'd be disturbing the earth beneath us," said Joe.

"Right," said Sarah. "And today, there's a mining company fracking for shale gas."

"These creatures must live deep underground," said Joe. "Now and again something forces them up to the surface. Something disturbs them and they crawl out to see what's going on."

"That's what I think, too," said Sarah. "Left alone, they stay underground."

"All these reports from the past," said Joe. "The disturbances were only temporary. But this fracking could go on for years. They'll be coming up to the surface all the time!"

"And in the past," said Sarah, "there weren't many people living in this area. Even in 1955, the main part of town was still over a mile away. Today, there must be hundreds living right on top of these creatures' home."

Joe looked up. "We have to warn them at the drilling site."

They hurried out of the house and down Oakshot Road. The entrance to the site used by the mining company was filled with vehicles. There were official cars used by the town's mayor and the local MP. There was a large van used by a news crew from the local TV station.

A group of protesters was gathered at the entrance, too. Security guards and police were stopping all unauthorised people from entering the site.

"We'll never get in," said Joe.

From where they were standing, Joe and Sarah

could see a collection of officials gathered beside the main drilling rig. The site foreman was being interviewed on camera. Everyone was wearing hard hats and high-vis jackets.

Behind them the drilling continued. Suddenly, the noise of the drill was drowned out. From the edge of the wood, a howling cry sounded.

CHAPTER 5

A goblin scurried into view at the far end of the site. Then another. Then another, and another. Soon, a swarm of the creatures was leaping and running in all directions.

The protesters at the entrance screamed in fright. Most dropped their placards and fled. Workmen inside the site ran, too. The officials and the site foreman stood frozen in disbelief for a moment. Then they, too, rushed for cover.

The news camera was turned towards the creatures. The goblins were avoiding the main drilling rig as it was brightly lit. They scuttled around the large pool of light. The man carrying the news camera didn't notice that one of the creatures was rushing up behind him. He screamed as it toppled him over. The camera smashed on the ground.

Sarah turned to Joe. "If we can shift those lights by the drilling rig we can drive them back, the same way we did last night."

"Right," nodded Joe.

The security guards and police were no longer taking any notice of the site entrance. Most of them were arming themselves with whatever they could. There was soon a battle raging between the police and the creatures. The creatures were winning. They slashed at the humans with their claws.

Joe and Sarah dashed towards the drilling rig. The site foreman was there, standing terrified under the glare of the lights.

"Get these lights pointing at the woods!" cried Joe.

The site foreman shook his head. Sweat ran down his face. "No way. We're safe in the light. They're coming from the hole. I should have listened!"

"What are you talking about?" asked Sarah.

"My men found a hole in the ground the other day. Just inside the woods. Like a large rabbit's hole. They said it looked odd. Wasn't there before. Fresh. Dug from underneath. I said, leave it. But that must be where they're coming up! I'm going to get explosives from the hut over there and I'm going to blow it up! Seal them in! Stop them forever!"

"No!" cried Joe. "Just stop the drilling. They'll go home."

"Can't!" cried the foreman. "Too much money at stake. No, just deal with these horrors. Seal the hole! Seal them in!"

He ran off before Joe or Sarah could stop him. He ran towards a small hut nearby where the mining company kept explosives used to start off the drilling. Joe and Sarah lost sight of him in the confusion.

The creatures were attacking in force. Some of the police had found heavy metal bars amongst the drilling equipment and were swinging them at the creatures like baseball bats. The goblins were fighting back fiercely.

The lights around the drilling rig were fixed onto tall stands. They could be turned using handles fixed to the back of them. Joe and Sarah each took hold of one. They directed the wide, bright beams wherever they saw one of the creatures.

The goblins hissed and wailed whenever the beams struck them. They screwed up their pale eyes and scuttled back into the darkness. One by one, they were sent scurrying for the safety of their burrow.

"I think it's working!" called Joe. "They're all heading back!"

"At least if we can send them back underground for now," called Sarah, "then we can – "

Suddenly, there was a gigantic flash of light from the direction of the woods. A thunderous bang echoed around the drilling site. The ground shook. Most of the lights toppled over on their stands and smashed. The humans who were still in the area cried out in alarm.

"The foreman," said Joe. "He got hold of the explosives after all."

More police turned up, along with several ambulances. At the edge of the wood, a crater was found. The hole the creatures had dug to reach the surface had caved in. They were sealed up underground once more. No trace of the site foreman was ever found.

A few days later, Oakshot Wood had returned to normal. The fracking had been stopped and the drilling site closed down.

Joe and Sarah felt that they would never return to normal, ever again. Everyone at school wanted to hear about what had happened that night. Media reports about the incident were dismissed as exaggeration or scare-mongering by those who hadn't been there.

Meanwhile, in the loneliest, darkest part of the wood, the soil began to stir. After a few moments, a claw broke the surface.

THE END